Happy Birthday, Sam

Happy Birthday, Sam

by PAT
HUTCHINS

THE BODLEY HEAD

London

OTHER PICTURE BOOKS
BY PAT HUTCHINS

Changes, Changes
Clocks and More Clocks
Don't Forget the Bacon!
The Doorbell Rang
Good-Night, Owl!
King Henry's Palace
One-Eyed Jake
One Hunter
Rosie's Walk
The Silver Christmas Tree
The Surprise Party
Titch
Tom and Sam
The Very Worst Monster
Where's the Baby?
The Wind Blew
You'll Soon Grow into Them, Titch

British Library Cataloguing
in Publication Data
Hutchins, Pat
Happy birthday, Sam.
I. Title
823'.9'1[J] PZ7.H96165
ISBN 0-370-30147-1

Copyright © Pat Hutchins 1978
First published in Great Britain in 1978 by
The Bodley Head Children's Books
an imprint of The Random Century Group Ltd
20 Vauxhall Bridge Road, London SW1V 2SA
First published by Greenwillow Books New York, 1978
Reprinted 1980, 1983, 1986, 1989, 1992, 1998
Printed in Hong Kong

For Sam

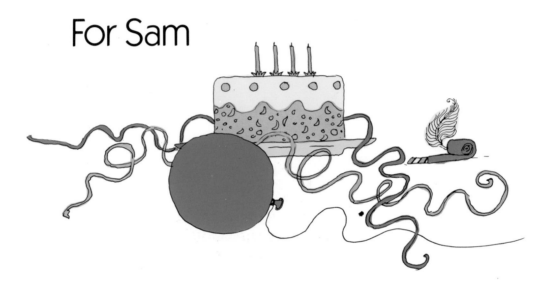

It was Sam's birthday.
He was a whole year older.

He climbed out of bed
to see if he could turn
the light on all by himself,
but he still couldn't reach
the switch.

He went to the wardrobe
to see if he could get
dressed all by himself,
but he still couldn't reach
his clothes.

He ran to the bathroom
to see if he could brush
his teeth all by himself,
but he still couldn't reach
the taps.

So he went downstairs.

"Happy birthday!"
said his mother and father,
and gave Sam a beautiful boat,
but Sam still couldn't reach
the sink to sail it.

"The postman's at the door,"
said Father, but Sam still
couldn't reach the knob
to open it.

"It's from Grandpa!"
said Mother and Father.
"What a nice little chair,
and just the right size."

"Yes," said Sam,
   and he took his little chair
   up the stairs,

switched on the light
in his bedroom,

took his clothes
out of the wardrobe
and dressed himself,

and went to the bathroom
and brushed his teeth.

Then he took his little
chair downstairs and sailed
his boat in the sink.
"It's the nicest boat ever,"
he said, "and the nicest
little chair."

And when Grandpa arrived for
the birthday party, Sam opened
the door and let him in.
All by himself.